A NOTE TO PARENTS

Reading Aloud with Your Child

Research shows that reading books aloud is the single most valuable support parents can provide in helping children learn to read.

- Be a ham! The more enthusiasm you display, the more your child will enjoy the book.
- Run your finger underneath the words as you read to signal that the print carries the story.
- Leave time for examining the illustrations more closely; encourage your child to find things in the pictures.
- Invite your youngster to join in whenever there's a repeated phrase in the text.
- Link up events in the book with similar events in your child's life.
- If your child asks a question, stop and answer it. The book can be a means to learning more about your child's thoughts.

Listening to Your Child Read Aloud

The support of your attention and praise is absolutely crucial to your child's continuing efforts to learn to read.

- If your child is learning to read and asks for a word, give it immediately so that the meaning of the story is not interrupted. DO NOT ask your child to sound out the word.
- On the other hand, if your child initiates the act of sounding out, don't intervene.
- If your child is reading along and makes what is called a miscue, listen for the sense of the miscue. If the word "road" is substituted for the word "street," for instance, no meaning is lost. Don't stop the reading for a correction.
- If the miscue makes no sense (for example, "horse" for "house"), ask your child to reread the sentence because you're not sure you understand what's just been read.
- Above all else, enjoy your child's growing command of print and make sure you give lots of praise. *You are your child's first teacher — and the most important one. Praise from you is critical for further risk-taking and learning.*

— Priscilla Lynch
Ph.D., New York University
Educational Consultant

To the real Ben
from the real Sis
—E.M.

Text copyright © 1996 by Eva Moore.
Illustrations copyright © 1996 by Meredith Johnson.
All rights reserved. Published by Scholastic Inc.
HELLO READER!, CARTWHEEL BOOKS, and the CARTWHEEL BOOKS
logo are registered trademarks of Scholastic Inc.

Library of Congress Cataloging-in-Publication Data

Moore, Eva.
    The day of the bad haircut / by Eva Moore ; illustrated by Meredith
Johnson.
        p.   cm.—(Hello reader! Level 2)
    "Cartwheel Books."
    Summary: Molly finally lets her mother cut her hair but is upset by
the results.
    ISBN 0-590-69770-6
    [1. Hair—Fiction.   2. Self-esteem—Fiction.]
    I. Johnson, Meredith, ill.   II. Title.   III. Series.
PZ7.M7835Day 1996
[E]—dc20   95-30062
                                                                CIP
                                                                 AC

12   1/0

                        Printed in the U.S.A.   24

            First Scholastic printing, December 1996

THE DAY
OF THE
BAD HAIRCUT

by Eva Moore
Illustrated by Meredith Johnson

Hello Reader! — Level 2

SCHOLASTIC INC.
New York Toronto London Auckland Sydney

Molly had a mother,

a father,

a brother named Ben,

a cat named
Charlie,

and a lot of nicknames.

Dad called Molly "My Little Lady."
Ben called Molly "Sis."
To Mom, Molly was "Sweet Girl."

One day Mom said,
"Sweet Girl, your hair is a mess.
You need a haircut."

But Molly said,
"No! I like my hair the way it is."

One week later,
Mom said,
"Sweet Girl, you really
do need a haircut."

But Molly said,
"No! I like my hair the way it is."

One week later,
Mom took Molly and Ben
to the barbershop.

Ben sat in the barber's chair.
Click! Click! went the barber's scissors.
Snips of hair fell to the floor.

"Good boy," the barber said.
He gave Ben a toy.

"See, Molly," Mom said.
"Don't you want a toy, too?"

But Molly said,
"No! I like my hair the way it is."

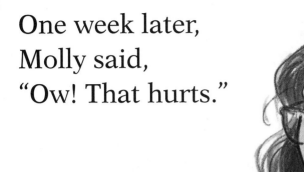

One week later,
Molly said,
"Ow! That hurts."

"Sweet Girl," Mom said,
"will you please let me cut your hair?"

And Molly said...

"Yes."

Click! Click! went Mom's scissors.
Snips of hair fell to the floor.

Mom cut a little more here . . .
click click click

and a little more there . . .
click click
and a little more . . .
click.

"Wait until you see
yourself, Molly,"
Mom said. "You look
so cute."

"It's too short!" Molly cried.
"Now I look like a boy!"

Mom looked at Molly in the mirror. "Yes," she said. "I guess some boys do have their hair cut like this."

"But I'm a girl," Molly said.
"Of course." Mom gave her a hug.

Molly went out onto the porch.
She felt very strange.

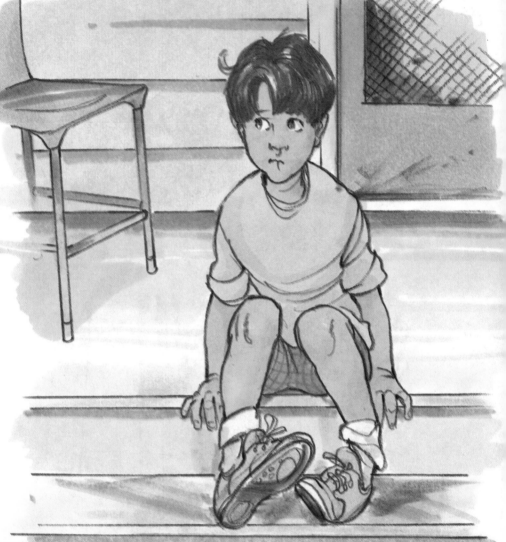

She was a girl,
but she had a boy's haircut.
What if people thought
she was a boy now?

Molly did not want anyone to see her.
She sat down in the corner.
The letter carrier came by.
He didn't see Molly.

Mrs. Green came by.
She didn't see Molly.

Molly's cat Charlie came by.

"Shhh, Charlie!" Molly whispered.
"You will give me away."

For a long time, no one else came by.

Molly was all alone.
She heard cars passing in the street.
She heard kids jumping rope.

Then—
THUMP THUMP

Molly heard footsteps
coming up the porch steps.

It was Ben.

"Hey, Sis," Ben said,

"what are you doing there?"

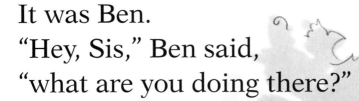

Molly began to cry.

"I'm hiding.
Mom cut my hair too short,
and now I look like a boy!"

"It's all right, Sis," Ben said.
"I will help you hide.
No one will get past me."

It was hard to stay still.
Molly wished she could
go out and play.

Then Ben called out,
"Look at that steamroller!
Some men are here to work
on the driveway next door.
Let's go watch!"

Molly stood and watched the big machine.
She loved the smell of the hot tar.
She loved the way the heavy roller
ironed out the piles of sticky gravel
and made a smooth black driveway.
She forgot all about her hair.

One of the workers saw them.

"Hi!" said Ben.
"Hi!" said Molly.
"Hi!" said the man.
"Do you boys live here?"

"No," Ben said.
"We live next door."

"And I am not a boy!" Molly said.
"I'm a girl with a bad haircut."

The man laughed.
"It's not so bad," he said.
"Besides, your hair will grow back
before you know it. It's about time
I had a haircut myself."

Molly ran home.

Mom said, "Here's my Sweet Girl.
I'm sorry about your hair."

But Molly knew
it did not matter.

She was still
Dad's "Little Lady,"
Ben's "Sis,"
and Mom's "Sweet Girl."
She always would be.